My Secret
VALENTINE

Patricia Hermes

A
LITTLE APPLE
PAPERBACK

SCHOLASTIC INC.
New York Toronto London Auckland Sydney

ISBN 0-590-48181-9

12 11 10 9 8 7 6 5 4 3 2 1   6 7 8 9/9 0 1/0

Printed in the U.S.A.   40

First Scholastic printing, January 1996

Contents

1

Late. Again.

"Watch me, Obie!" Katie Potts called to her twin brother, Obidiah. "Watch me slide."

"Hurry up!" Obie said, looking at his new watch.

"I'm hurrying," Katie said.

She put her notebook on the icy ground and sat on it like a sled. She gave herself a big, hard push. She slid right across their driveway and down the little hill by the garage.

She went so fast that at the bottom she tipped over backwards. She lay on her back

on the snow, looking up at the sky.

"Pretty neat, huh?" she said, as she sat up.

"It was fast," Obie said. "Four seconds. Now let's go. We'll miss the bus. Again."

Katie made a face. "We won't miss it," she said.

"Mom's waving at us," Obie said.

Katie stood up and brushed herself off.

Her mother was at the window, holding Baby-Child. Baby-Child's real name was Joshuah, but everyone called him Baby-Child.

Her older brothers, Matthew and Sam, were at the window with Mom and Baby-Child. Matthew and Sam hadn't been to school all week. Lucky ducks! They had chicken pox.

Mom was waving a hurry-up, get-going wave.

Katie waved back. Then she put her backpack down and sat on her notebook again, smiling to herself. Baby-Child can't do this, she thought.

Baby-Child can yell. Wet. Yell. Burp. Yell. Sleep. And yell.

He could get a gold star at yelling.

Hey, that's good! she thought.

The front door opened and Mom called, "Katie! Obie! Hurry or you'll miss your bus!"

"Told you," Obie said.

"We're going," Katie said.

She stood up and waved good-bye to Mom.

Mom was holding Baby-Child's hand, trying to make him wave, so she didn't see Katie waving.

Matthew and Sam didn't see, either. They were wrestling with each other.

"Bye, Mom!" Katie shouted.

Mom didn't hear. She had turned to separate Matthew and Sam.

Katie sighed. She put her backpack on, and turned her notebook over and looked at it. It was kind of smushed on the bottom now and some of her bear stickers were torn up.

She picked at one and scraped it off, sighing again.

"Baby-Child's a pain," Obie said quietly.

Katie looked at him. "I thought you liked Baby-Child?" she said.

Everybody liked Baby-Child. Everybody but Katie. Well, she didn't exactly *not* like him, but ever since he'd been around, things just were not the same.

"I do like him," Obie said. "Just not all the time."

Katie smiled. She took a nice, deep breath.

She and Obie turned the corner, heading for the bus stop. They passed Mrs. Anthony's house where there were Valentine's stickers on the front window.

"Hey!" Katie said, looking at Obie, her eyes wide. "When is Valentine's Day?"

"In February," Obie said.

"It's February now!" Katie said.

"Maybe it's today!" Obie said.

Katie rolled her eyes. "Not!" she said.

"We didn't get any valentines from Daddy. Besides, Mom always makes the cupcakes for school, and she makes me wear a red dress for Valentine's Day."

"What are you wearing now?" Obie asked.

Katie frowned. "I forget. But it's not a dress."

She stopped and opened her snowsuit jacket.

Blue overalls. And a blue-striped shirt.

"It's not Valentine's Day," Obie said.

"I knew that," Katie said.

But maybe Mom had forgotten about red dresses and cupcakes. Mom was busy with Baby-Child a lot. And she was busy with Matthew and Sam and chicken pox.

Katie and Obie passed Mrs. Moore's house.

There was a frozen puddle in the front yard.

"Look!" Katie said. "The puddle is frozen. I'm going to slide."

"Katie!" Obie said. "We'll miss the bus. Again."

Katie looked down the block.

No bus. "Just one more slide," she said.

"Hurry," Obie said.

Katie sat on the notebook again, and used her hands to walk herself along. She didn't slide fast like before, though, maybe because the ice was too lumpy.

She stood up just as a big yellow school bus rumbled by.

"Hey!" she yelled. "The bus. Our bus!"

Obie started to run. Fast. "Wait up, wait up!" he yelled.

Katie ran too, very fast. "Wait for us!" she yelled.

She could see the bus two blocks ahead, stopped, its red lights flashing.

Kids were getting on.

"Hey, wait up!" Obie yelled.

But the bus didn't wait up. The blinking lights went out and someone waved to them from the back of the bus. And then the bus pulled away.

"Uh-oh," Obie said. He stopped running and turned to look at Katie. "Now Mom will have to drive us. She'll have to hurry."

"Really hurry," Katie said. "Or we're in trouble. Big, big trouble."

Trouble

Katie and Obie hurried back home, Katie worrying about Mrs. Henry, their teacher.

Mrs. Henry was nice about everything, everything but late. Mrs. Henry hated late and she put people's names on the board if they were late. If your name went up on the board, it meant no recess.

Well, Katie thought, she'd just have to make sure Mom hurried now. *Really* hurried.

She and Obie burst into the house.

"We missed our bus!" Obie said.

"Can you drive us, Mom?" Katie said.

Sam looked up from where he was playing Power Rangers with Matthew. "Mom told you not to slide," he said.

Katie made a face at him. "Shush up," she said.

Mom just shook her head. "I'll do my best," she said. "But I told you not to dawdle before. Let's see, I have to put Baby-Child in his snowsuit and I have to find my keys."

She stopped and looked around at Matthew and Sam. "And you two have to get your coats and slippers on," she said.

"I don't need slippers," Matthew said. "The ice is *slippery* enough."

He laughed at his own joke.

Matthew always laughed at his own jokes.

Katie couldn't help laughing, too.

"I'll find your keys, Mom," Obie said.

He dropped his backpack and went in the kitchen.

Katie looked at Matthew and Sam. They were covered with spots, but they didn't act sick. They were sitting on the floor, making the Power Rangers bam against each other.

"Come on, Matt and Sam," Katie said to them. "Get your coats on or I'll be late."

Sam looked up and made a face at her. "Yes, MOM," he said.

Katie stuck out her tongue at him.

"Mom!" Sam said. "Katie stuck out her tongue at me."

Mom was holding Baby-Child under one arm, trying to slide her other arm into her coat. "Katie!" she said. She said it in her I-am-not-happy-with-you voice.

Sam grinned. Then he and Matthew went to get their coats and slippers.

Katie made a face at Sam's back.

"Katie!" Mom said.

Obie came in with the car keys. "I found them, Mom," he said. "On the high-chair tray."

He jiggled them in front of Baby-Child, who tried to grab them.

Mom shifted Baby-Child and hugged Obie with one arm. "What would I do without you, Obie?" she said.

She looked around then. "Everybody ready?" she said. "Get out to the car."

Matthew and Sam had their coats and slippers on and they ran outside. Through the window, Katie could see them jump into the car.

Obie went out, too.

"Ready?" Katie said to Mom.

"Oh, my!" Mom said. "How could I forget?"

She was looking down at Baby-Child, who was kicking his little fat feet. His little fat, *bare* feet.

"Katie!" Mom said. "Will you run upstairs and get him some booties, please?"

"Mom!" Katie said. "We'll be late."

"Please, Katie," Mom said. "It's cold

out! You don't want him to have cold little toes, do you?"

Maybe. But she ran upstairs anyway.

She found some booties on Baby-Child's changing table, blue ones with bunnies on them and furry trim.

"Mom," she said when she got down to the living room. "Could I get slippers with bunny fur on them someday?"

"You have slippers," Mom said. She laid Baby-Child on the sofa to put on his booties and, right away, he started to yell.

"I meant someday," Katie said, shouting to be heard. "Bunny ones?"

Mom didn't hear over Baby-Child's yelling.

"Hush!" Katie said to him. "Look!"

She wiggled her fingers in front of his face while Mom put his booties on.

Baby-Child stopped yelling. He gurgled. He grabbed for her fingers. He flipped right over.

"Katie, please!" Mom said, turning him onto his back again. "I'm trying to get his booties on!"

Katie folded her arms.

Mom pushed one of Baby-Child's fat feet into a bootie. "There!" she said.

Baby-Child waved his foot. Hard. It fell off. Not the foot. The bootie.

"These are way too small," Mom said, shaking her head. "Find a bigger pair, would you, Katie?"

"Mom, I told you I'm going to be late!" Katie said again. But again she ran back upstairs.

She looked through Baby-Child's dresser drawers.

She found booties, booties, booties. Before Baby-Child was born, Grandma and Great-Grandma had knitted fifty pairs at least. How many feet did they think this baby was going to have, anyway?

She picked out the biggest pair, yellow ones with no bunnies on them, and brought them down.

This pair went right on.

They went outside and got in the car, then put on their seatbelts and started off for school.

Late, Katie thought, as she watched the houses go by. She looked at Obie.

He was staring at his watch.

Was he thinking of no recess, too, just like she was? If there was no recess, she couldn't play with her best friend, Amelia Fritz.

No recess.

No best friend to play with.

Unless maybe, just maybe, they weren't late?

3

Whose Valentine?

At school, everything was quiet. The school yard was quiet, the playground was quiet, even the swings were not creaking in the wind.

The bell had rung and everyone was inside.

Katie opened the school door.

Inside, the hall was quiet, just like the playground had been.

She took a deep breath and looked at Obie.

He put a finger to his lips.

Together they tiptoed down the hall to Mrs. Henry's room.

Inside the room, people were standing by their desks, saying the Pledge. The new girl, Tiffany Bianca, was holding the flag perfectly straight and still. Everyone had their hands on their hearts.

Katie and Obie tiptoed in, and stood just inside the door, quiet as mice.

When the Pledge was over, everyone sat down, everyone but Katie and Obie. They tiptoed down the aisle to their desks.

"Just a minute!" Mrs. Henry said behind them. "This is the second time you two have been late this week."

Katie stopped tiptoeing and turned to Mrs. Henry.

Obie turned, too.

"What happened?" Mrs. Henry asked.

"Sliding," Obie said, sadly. "We were sliding."

"Our baby had to get his booties on," Katie said at the same time.

Mrs. Henry raised her eyebrows at Katie.

Katie felt her ears get hot, but she looked right back at Mrs. Henry. It was true. Baby-Child slowed everything.

"All right," Mrs. Henry said, "but you know there'll be no recess today." She sounded sad. "Now, go and sit like the good children I know you are. We have a fun project today."

Katie went to her seat by the cubbies, and Obie went to his by the windows.

When Katie passed Tiffany Bianca, Tiffany made a face.

Katie pretended not to notice, but her ears got hotter.

Tiffany Bianca was new to school — new and a big pain. She was never late. She never forgot her snack money. She never, never forgot anything, because Tiffany Bianca was perfect.

A perfect pain.

Hey, another good one, Katie thought.

She smiled, but she didn't feel happy. She hated no recess.

Mrs. Henry called on Katie's best friend, Amelia Fritz, to pass out red construction paper.

Amelia was the Paper Person this week. Katie liked being the Paper Person, but second best was for her best friend to be Paper Person.

Katie didn't have a special job this week.

She looked across the room to the gerbil cage. Anthony and Jennifer were the gerbils' names, but she couldn't see them in their cage from here. She knelt in her seat to see better.

"Everyone sit up straight and tall," Mrs. Henry said. "Are you listening, Katie?"

Katie looked away from the gerbils and up at Mrs. Henry. She unfolded her legs and tried to make herself very straight and tall, because she wanted to be Mrs. Henry's friend again — even if she had been late.

"Now, who knows what this month is?" Mrs. Henry asked.

Katie knew. February. She raised her hand.

"February!" Tiffany Bianca called out.

"That's right, it's February," said Mrs. Henry. "And what . . ."

"No fair!" Katie said. "Tiffany didn't raise her hand."

Mrs. Henry smiled. "And you didn't raise yours just now, either," she said.

Katie looked down at her desk and felt her ears get hot again.

"Now who knows what's special about February?" Mrs. Henry said.

Emil Marks was waggling his hand hard.

"Yes, Emil?" Mrs. Henry asked.

"Vacation!" Emil answered. "Winter vacation! My grandma is taking me to Minneapolis."

"That's nice, Emil," Mrs. Henry said. "What else happens in February?"

Katie folded her arms. She knew. But she wasn't going to tell now.

Margaret Anne Ericson was waving her hand and leaning out of her seat.

"Yes, Margaret Anne?" Mrs. Henry said.

"My mother's going to have a baby in February," Margaret Anne said.

"Well, that's nice, too," Mrs. Henry said. "But I was thinking of holidays. What special holidays do we have in February?"

Valentine's Day. And Presidents' Day. And Black History month — Katie's grandma had told her that.

She bet no one else knew that.

But she still wasn't going to tell.

Lots of people were waggling their hands.

Tracy Minton was whispering, "Call me, call me, call me!"

Mrs. Henry was looking at Katie. "Katie?" she said. "You look like you know something."

Katie nodded.

"Will you tell us?" Mrs. Henry said.

Would she?

She looked at Mrs. Henry, who was smiling at her.

All right.

"Valentine's Day," Katie said. "February is Valentine's Day and Presidents' Day. And I know something else. February is Black History month!"

"Very good, Katie!" Mrs. Henry said.

"There's something else, too!" Tiffany Bianca called out.

"You didn't raise your hand," Mrs. Henry said.

Katie turned and smiled at Tiffany, a not-nice smile.

Tiffany made a mad face back.

"Now, boys and girls," Mrs. Henry said. "For Valentine's Day, I'd like you to make a card for someone who might be lonely and maybe wouldn't get any cards. You could be their secret valentine."

Everyone was very quiet.

No cards? Who would get no cards for Valentine's Day?

Katie chewed on a piece of her hair.

Who did she know who didn't get any cards?

She looked around the room at the children, at Mrs. Henry . . .

Suddenly, she had an idea. A *perfect* idea. She knew exactly who needed a card.

And she would be the only person who had thought of it.

She smiled to herself and bent over her red paper.

Even without recess, this day might not be so bad.

4

The Dumb Time-out Chair

The lunch line lady would be her secret valentine.

Her name was Mrs. Torride, but everyone called her Mrs. Horrid. She checked that you ate your whole lunch before you turned in your tray. She made you eat the lunch vegetable every day, even if it was creamed corn. And she wouldn't let you trade lunches, not even a single cookie.

But once when Katie had no lunch recess because she had accidentally pushed in line, Mrs. Torride brought her a brownie. Then she sat at the table with Katie and told her all about her grandchilden while the other children played outside.

She would make Mrs. Torride the best Valentine's card ever.

There were sparkles and colored pencils and Magic Markers and scissors on the art table. There were lace and glue and magazine pictures there, too. And there were red construction paper hearts already cut out.

Katie got glue and silver sparkles and a green Magic Marker. She was going to make her own picture of a heart. It would be the best heart ever. And Mrs. Torride would be the gladdest person in the school.

Katie brought everything back to her seat.

Her friend Amelia got the exact same sparkles and Magic Marker as she did. She brought them back to her desk next to Katie's.

They smiled at each other.

They were allowed to talk during art projects if they kept their voices down. So Katie kept her voice very down.

"Who is your card for?" she asked quietly.

"Dr. Rick, my doctor," Amelia said. "Nobody likes doctors."

I do, thought Katie. But she didn't want to make Amelia sad, so she just said, "Oh."

"Oh, *what?*" Amelia said, kind of mad-sounding.

"Oh, *nothing!*" Katie said back, and she smiled at her friend.

Then she bent over her construction paper. Very carefully, she drew half of a heart, like a "C." Then next to it she drew another half of a heart, like a backward "C."

She held it away from her a little and frowned at it. It didn't look exactly like a heart. Actually, she thought, it didn't look *anything* like a heart. It looked exactly like a dented circle.

She peeked over at Tiffany Bianca's desk.

Tiffany had made a perfect heart. She was gluing on lace now, all perfect and

straight lace on her perfectly perfect heart.

Tiffany looked at Katie's card.

"Green and red isn't for Valentine's," she said. She kept her voice down, too, but it was a mean voice and when she smiled, it was a mean smile. "Green and red is for Christmas!" she said.

Katie covered her paper with her hand.

"It can be Valentine's, too," she said.

"Cannot," Tiffany said.

"Can," said Katie.

She felt a little worried, though. What if Tiffany was right?

She knelt up in her seat and looked around the room. Had anyone else used red and green?

Next to her, she saw Amelia get up and go to the art table. She came back with a black Magic Marker.

Who cared? Mrs. Torride wouldn't. She'd like green just fine.

Katie turned her paper over and started over again on the back, drawing a new heart there. Mrs. Torride wouldn't care if there were two hearts on her card, even if one of them was dented — and both of them were green.

But how did Tiffany make such perfectly shaped hearts?

She peeked at Tiffany's card again.

Tiffany had finished with the decorations, and was doing the writing.

"FOR MRS. TORRIDE WITH LOV," it said.

"Hey!" Katie said. "I'm doing one for Mrs. Torride!"

"I'm doing it!" Tiffany said. "And you're not supposed to peek."

"You peeked," Katie said. "You peeked and said red and green was just for Christmas."

"I know," Tiffany said. "It is."

"Who made that dumb rule?" Katie asked.

"My mother. She said so," Tiffany said. "My mother is an artist and she knows everything about colors."

"Your mother is a blab-face," Katie said.

"Mrs. Henry!" Tiffany stood up. "Mrs. Henry! Katie called my mother a name."

"Hush up!" Katie hissed at her.

Mrs. Henry came down the aisle to them. "Katie?" she said. "Is that true? Did you say something bad about Tiffany's mother?"

Katie didn't look up, just kept staring down at her card.

The card was ugly. The first heart was dented and the second heart was lumpy, and they were both green. Green and lumpy and ugly. Mrs. Torride would hate it.

Mrs. Torride would love Tiffany Bianca's perfect lace heart.

Katie crumpled up her card into a little tiny ball and stuffed it in her desk.

"Katie?" Mrs. Henry said. "I think a little time-out would help."

Katie still didn't look up.

"Come," Mrs. Henry said. She said it

nicely, but still Katie could feel tears coming up to her eyes.

She stood up. She hated time-out.

Time-out meant you had to sit in a dumb chair and take dumb time to dumb think.

It was where bad kids had to sit.

Katie had sat there three times already this week.

She followed Mrs. Henry to the time-out chair. Out of the corner of her eye, she saw Obie looking at her, a sad look.

She didn't look back, just kept her head down. She had made an ugly Valentine's card. Mrs. Henry was mad at her. And now she had to sit in the bad kids' chair.

She blinked back tears.

And she wasn't even really a bad kid.

Nothing Good to Eat

. Next day was Saturday, the best day in the week. There was no school. And Katie had her dad all to herself. They always started by going to McDonald's for breakfast.

This Saturday she was dressed and waiting when Dad came downstairs, before anyone else was up. Even Baby-Child was still asleep.

"Hey, Toots!" Daddy said. He came to her and mussed her hair. "Where to today?"

That was part of their Saturday, too.

They pretended like Daddy didn't know where they were going.

Katie played the game back.

"I think we should go to McDonald's," she said.

This time, though, Daddy made his face into a frown.

"Let's talk about it in the car, shall we?" he said.

"What's to talk about?" Katie asked, when they were in the car and driving.

"Well," Daddy said, using his serious voice. "Mom and I both had our checkups with Doctor Rick this week. We're fine, but Doctor Rick thinks we have too many fats in our diets. He says even children have too many. So I've been thinking we should try to avoid fats, like in bacon and french fries."

"Avoid them?" Katie said. "You mean like not eat them?" She made her eyes wide.

"Well," Dad said. "I guess I meant like not eat them all the time." And then he said, "We'll start today, all right? I thought we'd go to the diner. They have oatmeal there, and I know how you love oatmeal."

"Not on Saturdays," Katie said, but she said it very quietly.

Dad was pulling into the parking lot of the diner.

"Ready, Toots?" he said, turning and smiling at her.

She bent her head so he wouldn't see her face. If she had a lump in her throat, would he know?

When she got out, though, she took his hand.

At the table, Dad ordered oatmeal for both of them, oatmeal and whole-wheat toast and milk.

She ate the oatmeal and she didn't talk much.

"Something wrong, Toots?" Dad said, when they got back in the car.

Katie shook her head.

At the market, Daddy got the cart and took out the list.

"I'm going to cereals," Katie said.

She hurried away. Each week she was allowed to pick one box of sugar cereal for the family — but just one.

She was deciding which one when Daddy came around the corner with the cart.

"Hey, Toots!" he said, smiling at her. "How about skipping the sugar cereal? What do you think?"

Katie folded her arms and squinched up her eyes. "Froot Loops," she said. "That's what I think. Froot Loops."

"I think not," Daddy said softly. "Too much fat."

"I think *so!*" Katie said. "And fat is good for you!"

She made her face mean like a witch.

"Katie!" Daddy said. He used a stern voice.

"Daddy!" she said back, using the same tone of voice.

"I don't like that tone of voice, Toots," he said.

I don't like yours, either, she told him. But she said it inside her head.

He reached out and ruffled her hair. "Tell you what," he said, in his I-want-to-be-friends voice. "Valentine's is coming. Maybe for Valentine's Day you can get sugar cereal. We'll get it next week."

Big deal, she said.

But she said that inside her head, too.

She blinked hard. Nothing was right today. Or yesterday. Or the day before. Nothing, nothing, nothing.

6

Do Not Disturb

When they got home that day, Katie went straight to her room and closed her door, but first she put a big sign on it.

DO NOT DISTERB, the sign said. THIS MEANS YOU!!!

Then she lay down on the floor and pulled out her secret diary from under the bed. Daddy had given it to her for her birthday and it had a little key, to keep snoopy brothers out.

She would tell her diary everything that was wrong.

But when she went to open the diary

it was locked — and the key was missing! Missing!

And then she remembered: She had hidden the key in a secret place just last week, so her brothers couldn't read the diary.

Where, though? She couldn't remember.

She remembered hiding something inside a book. But what book? And was it the key she'd hidden there or something else? She thought something else. She thought maybe it was the note home from Mrs. Henry the second time she'd had to sit in the time-out chair.

She looked through her books. She looked in the toy box. She searched under the bed, under the pillow, even in her backpack.

No key. She had forgotten her secret hiding place.

Lost! It was lost.

Downstairs, she could hear one of her brothers laughing and Baby-Child squealing.

She went to her desk, got out a piece of notebook paper and a huge black crayon, and lay down on the floor.

She wrote:

List of everything
   that is Rong:

No-fat diets. Stopid
No Mcdonalds. Relly
Relly stopid. Kids need
Mcdonalds.
The time-out chair. And Im
not even a bad kid.
No Reces. Just becuse I
was late becuse of baby-
child.
Sam. He is a big fat brat.
Baby-child. He is stopid.
His feet are too big and he
makes me late.
Ugly Valentines.
TIFFANY.

She could have gone on with lots more, except there was a knock at her door.

"Go away!" Katie said. "Can't you read? It says *do not disturb!* And that means *you*, whoever you are!"

"Even me?" Daddy called through the door.

"Yes, you," she said.

But she got up and opened the door. Before she did, though, she stuck her list under the bed.

She stood at the door, her fists balled up on her hips. "What?" she said.

"Can I come in?" Daddy said.

She made a face, but she nodded and stepped back so he could come in.

"Can I sit down?" Daddy asked.

Katie nodded.

Daddy crossed the room and sat on the bed.

He patted the space beside him, like he wanted her to sit there, but she pretended not to notice.

"You're mad at me?" Daddy said.

Katie shrugged.

"How come?" Daddy said.

She shrugged again.

"Because of the nonfat diet?" Daddy said.

"Maybe," Katie said.

"Anything else?" Daddy asked.

Katie knelt down on the floor, and pulled the list out from under the bed.

She held it out to him, and he read it.

He looked up at her. "What's the time-out chair?" he asked.

"It's where bad kids have to go and sit," Katie said, folding her arms and glaring at him. "And I am not a bad kid."

"I know you're not," Daddy said.

"I know, too," Katie said.

"And Baby-Child is being a pain?" Daddy asked.

Katie nodded. "Sam, too," she said.

She could feel her lip quivering and she turned away.

Daddy was quiet for a long, long time.

"You know what?" Daddy said. "I bet

you could make some of these things better. Maybe not all of them, but some."

"Ha!" Katie said. But she turned back to him.

"Really," Daddy said.

"Like what?" Katie said.

"Why don't we go for a walk and talk?" Daddy said. "Maybe we can get ice cream."

Katie squinched up her eyes at him. "How come?" she said. "Doesn't ice cream have fat or something in it?"

Daddy smiled and shrugged. He stood up and held out his hand to her. "A little fat, maybe," he said. "But you know what? A little fat can actually be good for you."

Katie smiled, too. She took his hand.

"Told you," she said.

7

Big Pig

By Monday morning, Katie had made some promises to herself.

She and Daddy had had a long walk and a long talk. And Katie thought maybe he was right about some things. Like, maybe she could leave earlier for school so she wouldn't be late and miss recess. And Daddy said that maybe for Valentine's Day he'd get her a pretty ring. That way, if she kept looking at it on her hand, it might remind her to not call out without raising her hand. And she wouldn't call Tiffany or Tiffany's mother any more names. And she could make a new valentine. And if she couldn't draw hearts, she could always use cut-out ones like Daddy said.

All that stuff was easy to do.

Harder was not to fight with Sam no matter how mad he made her. And hardest yet was to not get mad about no fat.

Neither she nor Daddy mentioned the hardest of all — Baby-Child.

Katie knew why, too. They were stuck with him and that was that.

That night, she went to bed feeling happier than she'd felt in about forever. Soon, she'd be as perfect as Tiffany Bianca, and soon everyone at home and at school would notice. They might even notice her as much as they noticed Baby-Child. Even though Baby-Child didn't have to be perfect. He just got noticed no matter what he did.

On Monday morning, she and Obie left for school super early so they wouldn't miss the bus. They actually had to wait at the bus stop for ten whole minutes. She knew because Obie kept looking at his watch and he told her so.

At school, Mrs. Henry had more art projects planned. First they could finish their valentines. Then they could make brown paper hatchets to paste on the windows for Presidents' Day.

"Who knows why we make hatchets for George Washington?" Mrs. Henry asked.

Tiffany Bianca's hand shot up.

So did Irma Wagner's and Todd Racer's.

Mrs. Henry picked Todd.

"Because," Todd said, "George Washington cut down a cherry tree with a hatchet when he was a little boy and he wasn't supposed to, but he did and he told about it. He was honest."

"That's right, Todd," Mrs. Henry said.

Katie put her hand up and waited to be called on. She felt very proud about waiting like that.

"Yes, Katie?" Mrs. Henry said.

"Did he get in trouble?" Katie asked.

"Well, no, I don't think so," Mrs. Henry said. "Because he told the truth. He said, 'I did it,' when his father asked."

"You mean if you tell the truth, you don't get in trouble?" Katie asked, frowning.

"Mostly, that's true," Mrs. Henry said, smiling.

Katie knew Mrs. Henry always told the truth, but she was pretty sure Mrs. Henry was wrong about this.

But George Washington was a president. Maybe presidents could get away with stuff like that? Or maybe presidents were sort of like babies, and nobody got mad at them?

Anyway, now it was art time, and she'd do hatchets. But first, she'd redo her valentine — and she still had no idea about who to choose for her secret valentine. She couldn't give one to Mrs. Torride now, not if Tiffany was giving her a perfect one.

Katie sighed and looked around the room.

Everyone in here would get a valentine. There was already a big box in front. If you gave out valentines, the rule was you had to give one to each person in the class, even if you didn't like them. Teachers never said that, of course, about not liking other people. Teachers pretended that everybody liked everybody.

But then Katie realized that there was one person here who wouldn't get a valentine. Well, two persons. Except that they weren't really, actually persons.

She leaned across the aisle to Amelia. "Everybody we know gets valentines, right?" she said in her quiet voice.

Amelia nodded. "Don't you have a secret valentine yet?" She looked worried.

"Nope," said Katie. "But I have an idea."

"What?" said Amelia. She had cut out her hatchet and was now pasting little bunches of cherries on it.

"How about if I gave a valentine to

someone who isn't a real person?" Katie asked.

"A cartoon person?" Amelia said. "That would be pretty silly."

"No," Katie said. "I meant like somebody who isn't a person at all."

Katie looked around the room again, and saw that Tiffany was listening. She leaned closer to Amelia. "The gerbils!" she whispered. "I'm going to make a card for Jennifer and Anthony."

"Cool!" Amelia said, smiling at her. "I bet they won't get any cards."

"That's what I thought," said Katie.

She smiled and bent over her construction paper.

She drew two hearts on the front, side by side. They were a little crooked and lumpy again, but she knew Jennifer and Anthony wouldn't mind. Then she put lots of sparkles on the card. Next she covered it all over with lace, leaving room for the hearts to show. Then she drew a picture of a gerbil lying on a bed of straw in one heart. In the other

heart, she drew another little gerbil in another bed of straw. Except that when she held it away and looked at it, she thought they didn't look much like gerbils. They looked more like pigs. And the straw beds looked like plates.

She sighed. Baby pigs. Tiny baby pigs on plates.

"What's that?" Tiffany asked. "What's on your card?"

She was standing over Katie's desk, looking down at Katie's Valentine's card.

Katie put her hand over it. "Something," she said.

"What?" said Tiffany. "It looks like pigs. You're not supposed to put pigs on Valentine's cards."

"Says who?" Katie said. "And it's not pigs. So go away. Go sharpen your pencil. Or something."

"It is pigs," Tiffany said. "I can tell pigs."

Katie took a deep breath and glared up at Tiffany. With Tiffany standing like that, and Katie sitting, Katie could look right up Tiffany's nose.

"Actually," Katie said, smiling. "It is pigs. It's a picture of . . ."

Then, over Tiffany's shoulder, she saw the big clock on the wall. The clock that said almost time for recess.

It's a picture of you, Katie said. You and your turned-up pig nose. But she said it to herself, not out loud.

Because she wasn't going to miss recess.

So far today, she hadn't called out without raising her hand. She hadn't been late. And now, she hadn't called Tiffany a pig, not out loud.

Big pig, Tiffany, she said inside her head, and she smiled.

8

Yucky Brothers

When Katie got home that day, she felt very happy about school. And best yet, after school, now that Sam and Matt were finished having chicken pox, she could have Amelia over to play, the first time in a whole week. Amelia was also bringing her Barbie collection, and maybe she even could stay for dinner.

Katie hadn't asked Mom about the dinner part yet. But just in case Mom would say okay, Amelia had asked her mom the day before. She'd said yes.

Katie and Mom were waiting at the

door for Amelia that day. For once, Mom wasn't holding Baby-Child on one hip, and instead had her arm around Katie.

When Amelia came in, Mom shut the door and Katie and Amelia raced for the stairs, Amelia carrying her Barbie suitcase.

"Try to be quiet!" Mom called after them. "Baby-Child is down for his nap."

"What Barbies did you bring?" Katie asked, when they got to her room.

"All the ones I have," Amelia said. "Beach Barbie, Camp Barbie, Birthday Barbie, Skipper Barbie, and Ken."

Katie went to her toy shelf and got the little basket that had all the Barbie clothes in it, then went to her closet for her Barbies.

But there weren't any Barbies there.

She frowned and turned around. "I can't find my Barbies," she said.

Amelia just shrugged. "You can borrow one of mine," she said.

"I want mine!" Katie said. "Where could I have left them?"

"Downstairs?" Amelia said. "In the playroom?"

She was already undressing her Camp Barbie and putting some of Katie's Barbie clothes on it.

"Yeah, maybe," Katie said. "Want to come with me and look?"

"Okay," Amelia said. She finished putting a new outfit on Camp Barbie, with a little backpack and hiking boots, then stood up. "Ready," she said.

They went out in the hall, and as they passed the open door of Baby-Child's room, they could see him sleeping in his crib.

"Let's go look at him!" Amelia whispered.

Katie shrugged, but she and Amelia tiptoed in and stood looking down at him in his crib.

Katie had to admit Baby-Child was kind of cute when he was sleeping.

He lay on his back, one arm stuck out between the bars, the other one folded around his favorite toy, Big Bear. His face

62

was pink and round and he was breathing in and out with little soft puffs, and he twitched a little in his sleep.

"Watch this!" Katie whispered.

She bent to the side of the crib, and put one finger gently inside Baby-Child's hand.

His fat little fingers curled right up around hers.

She let him hold her for a minute, then gently slid her finger back out. "You try it!" she whispered.

Amelia did, but Baby-Child didn't grab her finger tight. He just sighed and twisted his hand away.

Funny, Katie thought. Maybe he knows who his sister is?

And then she and Amelia tiptoed out and went downstairs to the basement play-room.

Matt and Obie and Matt's friend Joey were playing Nok hockey, slamming the wooden puck hard with the wooden sticks, back and forth across the board.

At the big table where Katie played with clay and Barbies and stuff, Sam and his friend Arnold were playing — playing with Katie's Barbies!

The boys had put tiny toy rifles in the dolls' hands and were banging them against each other just like they did with the Power Rangers.

"Bam. You're dead!" said Arnold, banging Camp Barbie against Birthday Barbie.

"Bam to you!" Sam yelled, banging back with Beach Barbie.

"Stop it!" Katie shouted.

She raced across the room and grabbed at Arnold, who was closest. "Give them to me!" she yelled.

"I can play with them if I want!" he said, holding the Barbies up over his head.

But then he shrugged. He held out the Barbies and Katie grabbed them.

She turned to Sam. He was waving Beach Barbie by the ankles above his head, round and round in huge circles.

"Stop it! Give her to me!" Katie yelled, holding out her hand. "I'm telling Mom. Mo — om!"

Sam grinned and made a throwing motion, like he was going to throw Barbie clear across the room.

"Mo — om!" Katie yelled again.

Sam just laughed. He let Barbie drop from above his head, right down on the table, like he didn't care that she was a Barbie, practically a person.

And that's when Katie snatched up Barbie and hit him. Hard. Right over the head with Beach Barbie.

Just as Mom arrived in the playroom.

9

Not Fair

Amelia didn't get to stay for dinner. Sam had to have an ice pack on his head and had to go lie on the sofa. And Katie got sent to her room for the rest of the afternoon — to think about things! Mom said.

Katie sat on her bed, her arms folded. She wouldn't think, no matter what Mom said.

She didn't care if she was being punished, either. It was worth it. Sam had deserved it. But the truth was, she'd felt a little bit scared when she saw the blood. There hadn't been that much. But there was some, and Sam had suddenly gotten a very big lump that swelled up, right on the top of his head.

He had looked so surprised when she hit him.

So had his friend, Arnold.

But she bet they wouldn't touch her Barbies again. She smiled.

She was still sitting there smiling about that, when without even a knock, her door opened and her mom came in. Katie could tell by the look on Mom's face that it was going to be one of those big, long talks about how Katie could try to be nicer or better . . . blah, blah, blah . . . just like Dad had done.

And that's just what happened. Mom settled herself on the bed beside Katie as if she was going to stay all day. And she began to talk. On. And on. And on.

"Mom," Katie said, when Mom finally paused for a breath, "could you make cupcakes for the class Valentine's Day party again this year? It's Friday."

"Cupcakes?" Mom said. "We're talking

about your behavior with your brother."

"I know," Katie said. "But will you?"

Mom sighed. "Of course I will. I always do. But sometimes, Katie, I think I shouldn't. Sometimes I think you should be punished for your behavior to your brothers."

"But not that way," Katie said.

Mom screwed up her mouth, like she was trying not to smile.

"So you will, right?" Katie said. "The pink ones with red hearts? Even if Baby-

Child is being a pain, you'll have time to bake them on Thursday?"

Mom laughed and nodded. "Yes, I will. Now, about your brother and hitting . . ."

"He started it!" Katie said.

Mom reached out and brushed Katie's hair away from her face. "I know," she said. "He shouldn't have been playing with your toys without your permission. But that's no reason . . ."

"Playing with them!" Katie said. "He was killing them, Mom! Beach Barbie and Camp Barbie, they got all banged up!"

Mom sighed and rubbed her forehead. "Couldn't we have just one day when everyone is nice to everyone else?" she said.

So the next day, Katie tried again, very hard. That day was going to be special at school because it was the day they would mail their secret valentines. Each person was supposed to bring in a stamp and an envelope and they would address them and leave them on Mrs. Henry's desk. She would take them to the post office after school.

Also, that day, they would get to choose who would bring what for the Valentine's Day party on Friday. Katie knew what she was bringing.

School was almost over the next day when Mrs. Henry finally asked for volunteers for the party.

Right away Katie raised her hand.

So did Tiffany.

And so did about every other person in the class. Even Emil, who lived with his grandmother who was about a hundred years old, even Emil wanted to bring something.

Katie wondered what a hundred-year-old person would make.

First Mrs. Henry picked Amelia.

"My mom said I can bring the juice," Amelia said.

Mrs. Henry smiled and wrote it down on her list. "But that's too much for one person to bring," she said, looking up. "Do we have another juice volunteer?"

All the hands went down, all but Emil's.

So Mrs. Henry wrote down Emil's name, too.

Katie thought that was all right. His grandma had come to Parents' Night, so she could probably walk to the store all right.

"Who else?" Mrs. Henry said, looking around the room.

Katie began wildly waving her hand, but Mrs. Henry didn't even see her. Instead, she picked Margaret Anne, maybe because Margaret Anne's face was so red she looked like she was about to explode.

Katie sighed and hoped she'd be called next.

"If my mom doesn't have the baby by Friday," Margaret Anne said, "she'll bake cookies!"

"Well, that's nice," Mrs. Henry said. "But isn't that a lot to ask of your mom when there's a new baby coming?"

Margaret Anne bent her head down.

Katie thought she saw tears in Margaret Anne's eyes. And she thought she knew why, too. Babies ruined so much.

"Margaret Anne?" Mrs. Henry said. "If you really want to, if your mom wants to, that would be very nice."

Margaret Anne nodded, but she didn't look up. "She wants to," she said quietly.

"All right," Mrs. Henry said. "Margaret Anne will bring in cookies. Anyone else? Or do we have enough food already with juice and cookies?"

Katie was shaking her head no, and madly waving her hand. Cupcakes! Every party had to have cupcakes!

Right next to Katie, Tiffany was sitting up straight and tall, her hand up. But she held her hand like she was a traffic cop, arm straight out and perfectly still, not waving her hand at all.

Katie took a quick look at her, and then did the same. Straight and tall. Don't wave.

Too late.

Mrs. Henry picked Tiffany.

"I'll bring the cupcakes!" Tiffany said. "My mother is the best cake decorator . . ."

"MY mother is!" Katie blurted out,

even though she knew she should wait to be called on. "My mother *always* does the cupcakes."

Mrs. Henry smiled. "Yes, Katie," she said. "I've heard. Your mother is wonderful at cupcakes. But it's nice to take turns. I think we should let Tiffany."

"But Mrs. Henry!" Katie practically wailed. "My mother already said she would. I asked her yesterday."

"That's very kind of her," Mrs. Henry said, smiling. "But she has a new baby, too, doesn't she?"

Katie made a big, huffy breath, then turned to look at Tiffany.

Tiffany was looking back, this big, bright smile on her face. This big, bright, I WON smile.

"Besides," Mrs. Henry went on, "it's nice to take turns, isn't it? Tiffany should have a turn. After all, Tiffany's new."

"Tiffany's a pig," Katie said.

This time, she said it out loud.

10

Sneaky, Peeky Teacher

Katie was lucky. The bus announcement came over the intercom at the exact same moment that she said Tiffany was a pig. So no one heard. But that was the only good thing. It was totally mean what Mrs. Henry had done.

When Katie got off the bus with Obie that day, she walked along quietly. Mean, mean, mean, she thought. Mrs. Henry is mean.

Obie was kicking a stone in front of him, scuttling it along, then catching up to it, then kicking it again. He kept looking at his watch to see how long each kick and catch-up took.

"Obie?" Katie said. "Who's your secret valentine?"

"Somebody," he said.

"Somebody who?" Katie asked.

"It's a secret," Obie said. "And if I tell it, it won't be secret anymore."

He did another kick.

"I won't tell," Katie said. "So it will be."

Obie sighed. "Okay," he said. "It's Baby-Child."

"Baby-Child?" Katie opened her eyes wide. "How come?"

Obie smiled. " 'Cause it's his first valentine. I want to give him his first one ever."

"Daddy will give him his first one ever," Katie said, kind of mad. "Daddy gives us all valentines! Anyway, it's supposed to be for someone who doesn't get any."

"Well, he'll only get one other," Obie said. He ran ahead, kicking at his stone again.

Baby-Child! Katie glared at his back.

Next day wasn't much better. Katie told Mom not to bother with baking cupcakes, and all Mom said was, "Just as well. Baby-Child's teething, so I'll probably have my hands full anyway."

And then, at school, all Tiffany did was brag and brag about how good her mother was at baking cupcakes and decorating, brag about how she had heart-shaped cupcake tins. Brag, brag, brag.

There was one good thing, though. When they were doing personal journal writing, Mrs. Henry called Tiffany up to her desk for something. And just accidentally, Katie got to see one little part of Tiffany's journal entry. It said:

Nobody likes me here. I don't have any friends. I wish I could go back home to Seever School and my friends, Stacy and Monnie and Missy.

Good! Katie thought. You have no friends because you aren't nice.

But when Tiffany came back and sat down, Katie took a quick look at her.

Did Tiffany really have inside feelings just like Katie did? Or was she just making up something to put in her journal the way Katie sometimes did?

Katie couldn't tell anything by looking at Tiffany, though. Tiffany just kept looking perfectly perfect. Happy, even.

And then Mrs. Henry called Katie to her desk.

Katie closed her journal, so sneaky Tiffany couldn't spy and read it, and then went up to Mrs. Henry's desk.

"Let's go out in the hall for a moment," Mrs. Henry said.

Uh-oh. Out in the hall meant trouble.

Katie followed Mrs. Henry, thinking. What could she be in trouble about? She thought of all the things she'd done and hadn't done. She hadn't called out without raising her hand. She hadn't done anything mean or fresh, so she hadn't had any time today in the time-out chair. And Mrs. Henry couldn't be mad about her calling Tiffany a name because she couldn't have heard. Besides, that was yesterday.

When they were standing in the hall, Mrs. Henry turned to Katie, looking very serious.

"Katie," she said. "You don't seem happy these days."

Katie shrugged. Happy? Had Mrs. Henry forgotten already about the cupcakes?

"Want to tell me what's wrong?" Mrs. Henry said.

No, Katie thought.

She looked at the floor.

"You never used to get in trouble, Katie," Mrs. Henry went on. "But you've spent more time in the time-out chair than anyone else this month."

No kidding! Katie thought. And who made me sit there? But of course she didn't say anything like that.

"And something else," Mrs. Henry

said. "Your valentine, your secret valentine?"

Katie looked up. "What?" she said, squinching up her eyes.

"I saw who it was for when I took it to the post office yesterday," Mrs. Henry said. "And I'm disappointed in you. The purpose of doing that card was to bring some happiness into someone's life. Couldn't you think of even one person who would be happy if you sent them a valentine?"

Katie folded her arms. "You said it should be for someone who wasn't going to get one," she said. She felt her eyes about to water. "The gerbils won't get one. Except now they'll get mine."

"The gerbils don't *need* one, Katie," Mrs. Henry said. "Everyone else in the class sent one to someone who would appreciate a card. Even your brother — he sent one to your baby."

And you read everyone's cards and you're a sneaky spy! Katie thought. A very sneaky spy! And Baby-Child doesn't need a card, and Obie is a brat. But she didn't say those things out loud, either. She had to blink hard to keep away the tears.

"I'm going to be calling your mom this afternoon," Mrs. Henry said. "I'm not calling to tell on you," she said. "I just want all of us to find out what's wrong and to help you. All right?"

Not all right, Katie thought.

Nobody cared anyway.

Still, she sighed. What could she do about it?

And then, suddenly, she knew. She knew just what she could do about it.

It almost made her smile.

11

Nobody Likes Me

She would not sneak away. She would run away. Nobody cared. They'd probably even help her to leave. Sam sure would.

It would be easy to do. She'd just pack her stuff. And if she went far enough away, she wouldn't even have to go to this school anymore. Maybe she could even go to Tiffany's old school, Seever School, where people were nice — if she could find out where that school was.

But then she sighed.

Seever School might be easy to find, but where could she live? She was pretty grown-up, but not enough to live on her own. She knew that you didn't just run away and live in the woods. You had to have some place to run away to, to live. But where?

And then she knew! Grandma and Great-Grandma! They lived together and they loved having her visit them. She even thought that maybe they didn't like Baby-Child so much themselves. Whenever they came to visit, Grandma whispered to Katie that babies were a big pain, taking everyone's attention. And Great-Grandma said they smelled something awful.

But Grandma and Great-Grandma lived pretty far away — all the way to the end of the bus line.

Still, she could do it. She'd get money from Mom and Dad, and they might even help her onto the bus and give her directions.

When she got home that day, she yelled hello to Mom, who was in the laundry room, then went right to her room.

And there on her bed was a new red dress with a fluffy white lace collar and puffy

sleeves and a skirt that was so full it would spin out when you turned around.

A note on the dress said, From Mom — for your Valentine's Day party tomorrow.

The Valentine's Day party. Tomorrow. She would miss the party if she ran away today.

Well, who cared about juice and cookies? And the cupcakes would probably be rotten anyway.

She picked up the dress and held it up in front of her in the mirror.

It was so pretty! And soft, too, sort of like velvet, like her green holiday dress. She wanted to run downstairs and tell Mom thanks, but decided to wait. Later. She'd talk to Mom later. And she'd pack the dress and take it with her to Grandma's.

She went to the phone then, the phone in Mom's room.

She dialed Grandma's number. When Grandma picked up the phone, Katie said, "Grandma, can I come live with you?"

There was quiet on the other end of the phone, a real long quiet.

"Grandma?" Katie said. "Did you hear me?"

"Well, I heard you, yes," Grandma said. "Of course you can come here. But do you really mean *live* with me? Or just visit?"

"Live," Katie said.

"Oh," Grandma said.

"So can I?" Katie said.

"Don't you think your mom and dad will miss you?" Grandma asked.

Katie sighed. She shook her head no.

"Don't you?" Grandma said again.

"No," Katie said — out loud. She still forgot sometimes that people couldn't see her on the phone. "They won't miss me."

"Oh," Grandma said.

"So can I come?" Katie said.

"Of course you can," Grandma said. "When should we expect you?"

Katie shrugged. "Dinnertime," she said. "I'll be there for dinner."

She looked at the clock on Mom's dresser, right next to the picture of her and Mom and Dad, taken on her very first day of school. It was already four o'clock.

"*After* dinner," she said. "Right after."

And then before she could change her mind, she hung up and went back to her room to finish her packing.

First, though, she took off her overalls, and tried on the dress.

Perfect! It was perfect! It fit just right, and the skirt did swish out when she spun around, just like she knew it would. She fixed the collar, pulling the lace till it was nice and straight, then tugged at the sleeves, puffing them up.

She stood straight and tall in the mirror, then twirled around slowly.

Boy, would Tiffany be jealous when she saw this dress. Unless Tiffany's mother bought her one that was even better.

Nah. There couldn't be a better one.

But Tiffany wouldn't see it.

She took off the dress, then folded it

carefully to put it in her backpack. Tomorrow, at Grandma's, she would wear it. Tomorrow, she wouldn't go to school.

She packed up all her things and then she was almost finished. She sat down on her bed.

One more thing to do.

A note. When you ran away, you always had to leave a note.

So she wrote one:

I'm running away.
Nobody likes me anymore.

12

Yes, They Do!

Katie didn't go downstairs until she was called for supper.

When she went down to the dining room, the boys were already seated around the table, with Baby-Child in his high chair at the end of the table. Dad was beginning to spoon out the lasagna.

Lasagna! Her favorite.

For once, the boys weren't all poking at each other and making noise. Only Baby-Child was hammering his spoon up and down on his high-chair tray.

"Hiya, Toots!" Dad said, looking up

and smiling at her. "I didn't even know you were home, you were so quiet."

"I was up in my room," she said.

She looked at Mom, who was tying a bib under Baby-Child's chin.

"I like my dress, Mom," Katie said quietly.

Mom looked up and smiled. "I'm glad," she said.

Katie sat down.

Daddy filled a plate with lasagna and handed it to Matthew, who passed it down the table to her.

"Here you are," Matthew said quietly.

He didn't even say one of his usual punny jokes, like how cheesy dinner was or anything.

Weird. What was wrong?

Across the table, Obie had a huge frown on his face so that he looked super mad. But she knew him and knew he wasn't mad. He always looked like that when he was worried.

And then she realized: Mrs. Henry must have called.

She snuck a quick look at Mom, but Mom didn't look particularly mad.

When they were all served, Daddy said the prayer, like he did each night. Only this night, the prayer wasn't the usual one, the thank you for the world so sweet and the food we eat and all. This night, Daddy said something different.

"Lord," he said, when everyone had bowed their heads, "thank you for each member of our family. Each one is important to us, and each one, we know, is important to you. May we all learn to appreciate this. Amen."

Everybody echoed "Amen," and then they all started to eat.

Except that Katie didn't feel too hungry.

After a while, she noticed that nobody else seemed hungry, either. Nobody except Baby-Child. He was shoving food into his mouth with his little curved pusher spoon —

into his mouth and onto his chin and even into his hair.

Everyone else just moved food around plates, not saying much.

Until finally Mom said, real quietly, her head bent over her plate as if she were talking to the lasagna, "Mrs. Henry called this afternoon."

Uh-oh!

"What did she want?" Katie asked, her voice kind of trembly.

"She said you've spent a lot of time in the time-out chair," Mom said.

"That's because she makes me!" Katie said.

Mom didn't answer, but she looked a little bit like she was trying not to laugh.

"And Grandma called, too!" Obie blurted out suddenly. His eyes were wide, and there were bright red spots high on his cheeks like he got when he was upset. "She said you called!"

"She did?" Katie said.

Well, she hadn't told Grandma not to

tell anybody. And anyway, everyone had to know. Might as well tell them now.

"Yes, I called her," she said. She took a deep, shaky breath and added, "I'm going to go live with her."

"You can't!" Obie said.

"Can!" Katie said. "Grandma said so."

"Then I'm going, too," Obie said, folding his arms and staring at her.

Next to Obie, Katie saw that Sam was turning his fork over and over, upside down, right side up. He looked up at her and then away.

Matthew was suddenly shoveling food into his mouth, fast, as if he had to get it eaten and over with in a hurry.

And Daddy — Dad was eating slowly, deliberately, not looking up, like he was counting the number of times he was supposed to chew each bite.

"I'm going right after supper," Katie said. "Actually, I'm all packed."

Daddy looked up then. "You are?" he said.

Katie nodded. "Yes. I'm all ready."

Daddy sighed. "Well," he said. "All right then."

Katie stared at him. All right? He'd let her go? Just like that?

She felt her eyes begin to sting.

"It's really all right?" she said.

Daddy shrugged. "If you've made up your mind," he said. "What can I do?"

You can say no, don't go. You can say you don't want me to. You can say . . .

She looked away. She felt her lip trembling, and she bit down on it.

"I've prepared a little extra lasagna," Mom said. "You can take it to Grandma."

Katie nodded.

"I didn't mean to bash up your Barbies the other day," Sam said, suddenly. "It was just a joke."

Matthew stopped shoveling in food and looked up then. "I like the way you laugh at my jokes," he said, and then he bent over his lasagna again.

"And you're my twin!" Obie said, mad-like.

Everyone was very quiet then for a long time.

Finally, Mom said, "The lasagna for Grandma is terribly hot. It might be hard to balance. Along with all your other things."

"And it's supposed to snow tonight," Daddy said.

"Yes, and Mrs. Henry said there's going to be a nice party at school tomorrow," Mom added.

"And you do have a pretty new dress to wear," Daddy said.

Were they trying to persuade her to stay?

"We love you very much," Mom said quietly. "We do."

"I do," Daddy said.

"Me, too," Matthew said.

"Yeah," Sam said. "Me, too."

"Me, too," Obie said.

"Me doo!" Baby-Child yelled.

Everybody laughed. Laughed and stared at Baby-Child.

Even Katie laughed. Had he really said that? His first words? Me, too? Love you?

He noticed everyone looking at him and waved his spoon. He banged it up and down on the high-chair tray. "Me, doo, me, doo!" he crowed.

"See that?" Daddy said. "Even Baby-Child loves you."

Baby-Child was grinning at her, his face covered with mushed-up lasagna and to-mato sauce.

Katie took a deep, trembly breath, and fought down the water that was coming to her eyes. Yeah. She loved him, too. Sort of. Loved them.

But something was still missing. And she didn't know what it was.

Until Daddy said it, and Mom, too, both of them practically at the same time — two things.

"Not only love you," Mom said. "We need you. Each and every one of us."

"Need you," Daddy said. "And we won't let you go."

Katie smiled and took a deep breath. That was it. Exactly what was missing. Just exactly what she needed to hear.

13

A Practically Perfect
Valentine

The next day was Valentine's Day, and when Katie put on her new dress and looked in the mirror, she knew she looked pretty, maybe as good as Tiffany. And when she came downstairs, Daddy gave her a Valentine's Day present, a gold ring with a tiny red stone in the middle. A perfectly beautiful gold ring!

She put it on, and even her brothers said it was pretty, although Sam did add, "Sort of." But he grinned when he said it and he didn't get mad when she poked him.

She and Obie left so early that they

had plenty of time to make the bus. And
then, when they got to school, they had
plenty of time to put their Valentine's Day
cards in the box with everyone else's. Katie
even had a card for Tiffany, but it was the
smallest one from the box of cards Mom had
bought for her and it said:

2 good
2 be
4 gotten.

Really stupid, Katie thought, but stupid was just right for Tiffany.

Amelia was in school early, too, and
right away, Katie showed her the ring.

"Oh, wow!" Amelia said. "Your dad
gave you that?"

Katie thought maybe Amelia looked a
little jealous.

Katie nodded. "Yeah, my dad," she
said.

Because he loves me, she thought. And

won't let me go. But of course she didn't say that out loud.

She and Amelia had just finished putting their cards in the card box when Tiffany came in. She wasn't wearing her regular snowsuit jacket, but was all dressed up in a red furry coat open over a red velvet dress. Her hair was pinned up to one side in a big curl with a huge red barrette that sparkled. And she was carefully holding a flat, oblong box. Cupcakes.

Right away, Katie went to her seat.

She didn't want to see the cupcakes, and she especially didn't want to hear the bragging.

Amelia sat down alongside her, first getting some construction paper and art supplies.

"I'm doing a card for Mrs. Henry," Amelia said when they got back to their desks. "I forgot her."

"I didn't forget her," Katie said.

But then she thought of another card, one she had forgotten — maybe never really thought of — Baby-Child.

Well, why not?

The bell hadn't rung yet, so there was still time for quiet art projects and for sharing time. She went back to the art supply desk, brought supplies to her own desk, and began making a Valentine's heart for Baby-Child, a heart that she decorated with zillions of sprinkles.

She shook the card a little so the extra would fall off, and then she put on some lace, gluing it all around the heart.

"That's pretty," Amelia said, looking across the aisle at it.

"Thanks," Katie said. She held it out to admire it herself. It was pretty! A lumpy heart, sort of, but pretty.

"I like it, too," Tiffany said.

Katie quickly put her hand over it and looked up.

Tiffany was standing on the other side of her desk, some pencils in her hand.

Katie didn't answer, just waited for Tiffany to go to the pencil sharpener before she uncovered the card.

Tiffany went, then came back and sat down. Jessica watched as Tiffany picked up one of her pencils and began doodling — little bitty hearts all over the cover of her notebook.

"How do you do that?" Katie said suddenly.

Tiffany looked over at her. "What?" she said.

"That," Katie said. "The hearts. How do you do them so good?"

"I don't know. I just do," Tiffany said. "Want me to show you?"

Katie shrugged. "Okay."

Tiffany leaned across to Katie's desk.

"Okay," she said. "Pick up your pencil."

Katie did, and Tiffany put her hand over Katie's hand.

"Like this," Tiffany said.

She guided Katie's hand over a piece of construction paper. Up. Curve around. Down. Up. Curve around. Down. With Tiffany guiding, they drew a bunch of hearts. They filled up the paper with them.

After a minute, Tiffany took her hand away. "Okay," she said. "You try it."

Katie did. Up. Curve around. Down. Up. Curve around. Down.

She held the paper out and looked at it.

"Cool!" she said, smiling at Tiffany. "Thanks."

"My mother isn't really an artist," Tiffany said suddenly. "I just made that up."

"Oh," Katie said.

"She works at Dunkin' Donuts," Tiffany said.

"She does?" Katie said.

Tiffany nodded.

"Are the cupcakes good?" Katie asked.

And then wondered why she'd bothered to ask that. Of course they were good. Perfect. Perfect Tiffany's perfect mother would make perfect cupcakes.

Tiffany shrugged. "I guess," she said. She looked down at her desk. "Want to see them?" she asked.

Not really.

But for some reason, Katie suddenly remembered that sneaky look she'd had into Tiffany's personal journal. No friends. Tiffany had no friends.

Katie stood up. "Okay," she said.

So they went up front to where Tiffany had put the cupcakes on the big front table, Tiffany leading, Katie behind.

Suddenly, Tiffany turned and smiled at Katie.

Not a mean smile.

Not a show-off one.

Just a regular smile, a nice one.

And Katie smiled back. Not a mean smile, either. A nice one.

But she couldn't help thinking about one very important thing — the cupcakes.

And she couldn't help hoping that they weren't exactly perfect.